The Christmas Kitten

Note

Once a reader can recognize and identify the 32 words used to tell this story, he or she will be able to read successfully the entire book. These 32 words are repeated throughout the story, so that young readers will be able to easily recognize the words and understand their meaning.

The 32 words used in this book are:

a	fly	kitten	the
alone	for	knows	time
bows	found	off	to
but	go	play	wants
can	home	ribbons	way
Christmas	in	Santa	what
come	is	snow	where
do	just	stay	you

Library of Congress Cataloging-in-Publication Data
Packard, Mary.
    Christmas kitten/by Mary Packard ; illustrated by Jenny Williams.
      p. cm — (My first readers)
    Summary: A little kitten wants to stay with Santa and Mrs. Claus on Christmas eve, but the workshop is too crowded so Santa finds a better place for it.
      ISBN 0-516-05364-7
      (1. Christmas—Fiction. 2. Cats—Fiction. 3. Santa Claus—Fiction.
      4. Stories in rhyme.) I. Williams, Jenny, 1939- ill. II. Title.
III. Series: My first reader.
PZ8.3.P125Ch 1994
(E)—dc20

94-12301
CIP
AC

The Christmas Kitten

Written by Mary Packard   *Illustrated by* Jenny Williams

ℂℙ CHILDRENS PRESS ®
CHICAGO

Text © 1994 Nancy Hall, Inc. Illustrations © Jenny Williams.
All rights reserved. Published by Childrens Press ®, Inc.
Printed in the United States of America. Published simultan
Developed by Nancy Hall, Inc. Designed by Antler & Bald
1 2 3 4 5 6 7 8 9 10 04 03 02 01 00 99 98 97

Christmas Kitten is alone.

6

Christmas Kitten wants a home!

Come in, Kitten.

9

You can stay.

Kitten wants to play, play, play!

But Christmas Kitten is in the way.

15

In the ribbons.

In the bows.

Where is Kitten?

20

Santa knows!

Christmas Kitten, time to go.

Time to fly off in the snow!

Santa knows just what to do!

Santa found a home for you!

ABOUT THE AUTHOR

Mary Packard is the author of more than 150 books for children. Packard lives in Northport, New York, with her husband and two daughters. Besides writing, she loves music, theater, walks on the beach, animals and, of course, children of all ages.

ABOUT THE ILLUSTRATOR

Jenny Williams was born and raised in London, England. She began her art career in London as well. She now lives in an old farmhouse in the countryside of Wales with her husband, two children, and dog. Williams enjoys reading, cooking, and country life, including the changing seasons. She loves to travel when she has time. Her work gives her so much pleasure that she considers it a hobby, too.